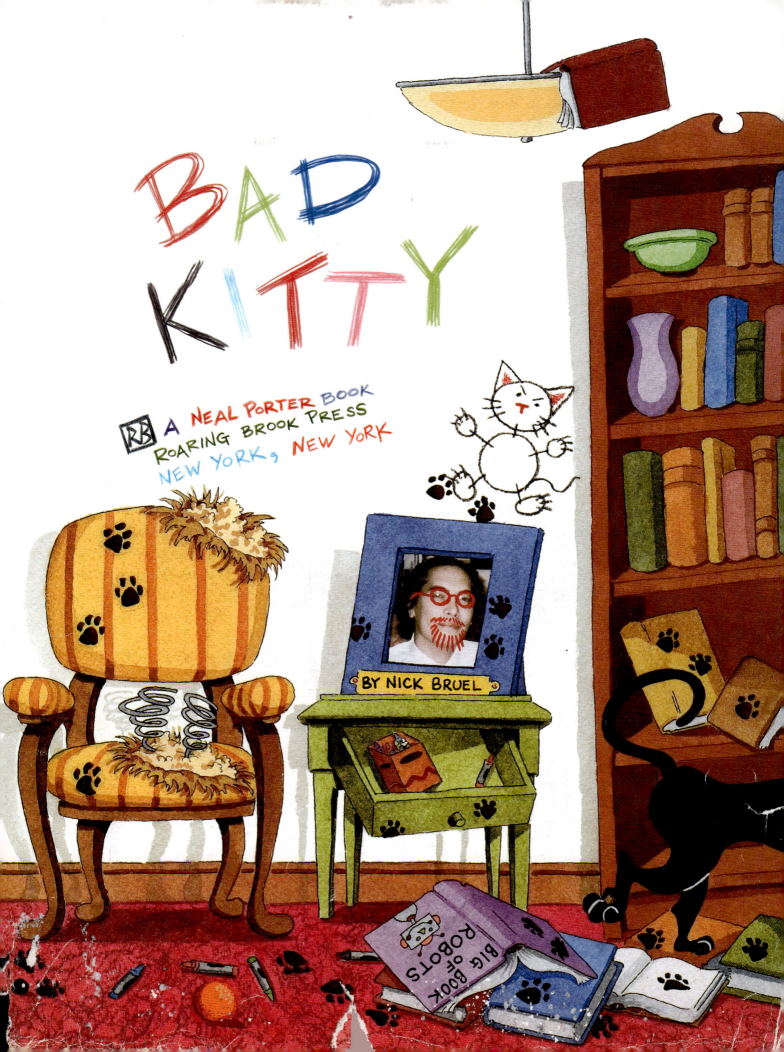

BAD KITTY

A NEAL PORTER BOOK
ROARING BROOK PRESS
NEW YORK, NEW YORK

BY NICK BRUEL

Text and illustrations copyright © 2005 by Nick Bruel
A Neal Porter Book
Published by Roaring Brook Press
Roaring Brook Press is a division of Holtzbrinck
Publishing Holdings Limited Partnership
175 Fifth Avenue, New York, New York 10010
www.roaringbrookpress.com

Library of Congress Cataloging-in-
Publication Data
Bruel, Nick.
Bad kitty / Nick Bruel.
p. cm.
Summary: When a kitty discovers
there is no cat food in the house, she
decides to become very, very bad.
ISBN: 978-1-59643-299-4
[1. Cats—Fiction.   2. Food—Fiction.
3. Behavior—Fiction.   4. Alphabet.]
I. TItle.
PZ7.B82832Bad 2005
[E]—dc22   2004024456

FOR CARINA

Anniversary ISBN 978-1-62672-245-3
First edition October 2005
Anniversary edition March 2015
Printed in China by South China Printing Co.
Ltd., Dongguan City, Guandong Province
10 9 8 7 6 5 4 3 2 1

She
wasn't
always
a
bad
kitty.

She used to be a good kitty,

until one day . . .

OH, DEAR!
WE'RE ALL OUT OF
FOOD FOR THE KITTY! ——

ALL WE HAVE ARE
SOME HEALTHY
AND DELICIOUS...

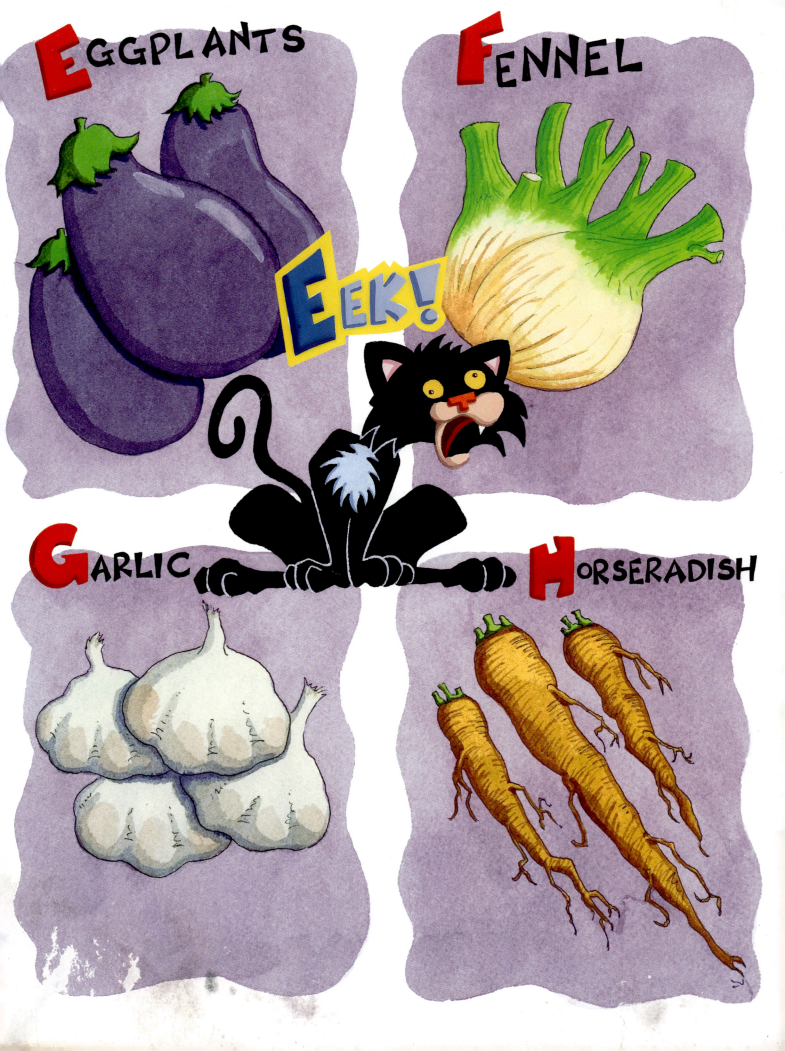

RH**U**BARB

VEGETABLE STEW

YUCK!

WATERCRESS

XIGUA

YAMS AND **Z**UCCHINI

Kitty was not happy.
Not happy at all.

That's when she decided she would be a BAD kitty.

But not just any bad kitty—a very, very, bad, bad, BAD kitty.

She . . .

ATE MY HOMEWORK

BIT GRANDMA

OH DEAR!

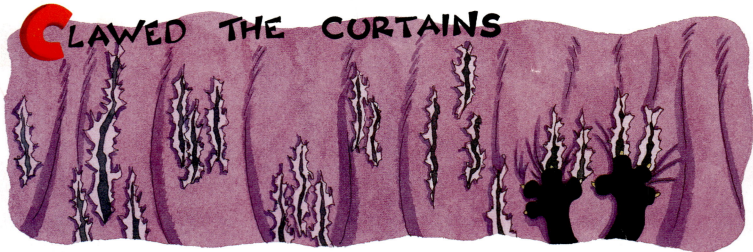

CLAWED THE CURTAINS

DAMAGED THE DISHES

ENDANGERED THE GOLDFISH

FLOODED THE BATHROOM

GRAPPLED WITH GUESTS

HURLED HAIR BALLS AT OUR HEADS

WAS **M**EAN TO MY MOMMY

WAS **N**ASTY TO DADDY'S NECKTIES

OVERTURNED HER CAT BOX

PLOTTED AGAINST US

QUARRELED WITH OUR NEIGHBOR

RUINED THE RUG

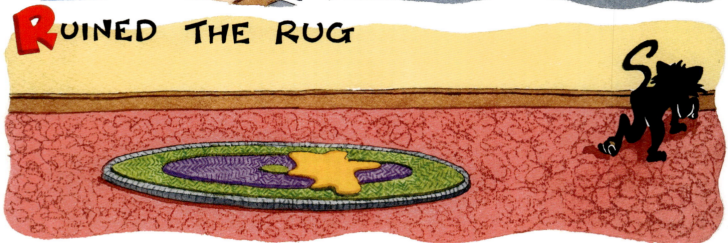

SOLD MY TOYS

TORMENTED A LITTLE MOUSE

But then . . .

I'M BACK FROM THE GROCERY STORE! LOOK AT ALL THE GOOD FOOD I BOUGHT FOR KITTY!

WE HAVE . . .

What a bad kitty.

What a very, very, bad, bad, bad kitty.

Now, kitty was happy!
Very, very happy!

She decided that from now on, she would be a GOOD kitty!

But not just any good kitty—a very, very, good, good, good, kitty!

She . . .

Uh-oh . . .

How can we reward such a good kitty?

I know . . .

LOOK, KITTY! WE'VE BROUGHT YOU A NEW FRIEND! YOU CAN PLAY TOGETHER, AND YOU CAN GO TO THE PARK TOGETHER, AND YOU CAN <u>SHARE</u> <u>YOUR</u> <u>FOOD</u> <u>WITH</u> <u>HIM</u>!

MOPPED THE BATHROOM

WAS **N**ICE TO MY MOMMY

SANG **O**PERA ALL NIGHT

BRAVO!
ENCORE!
MORE!
MORE!

WAS **P**OLITE TO THE VET

QUIT QUARRELING WITH OUR NEIGHBOR

REPAIRED THE CURTAINS

SAVED THE DAY

TIED MY SHOES

GAVE ME A **Y**ELLOW YO-YO

AND LULLED THE BABY TO SLEEP Z Z Z Z Z Z Z

What a good kitty!
What a very, very good, good, good kitty!

INVITED AFFECTION

JOINED THE JAMBOREE

KISSED THE GOLDFISH

LEFT THE LAMP ALONE

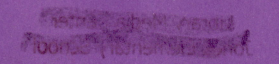